I0703406

Flower Princess And The Man With Magic Reed

A STORY OF TRUE LOVE

Written by Cyril Mukalel

Illustrated by Özgür Uguz

Potter's Wheel Publishing House
Minneapolis

Voices blaring, never hearing
Voices ignored, forever echoing
Voices desired, ever deserting

I heard a story of a voice
A voice infused with the sweet fragrance of a promise
A voice to strum my heart,
A voice to make me sing forever

My Love, if I never told you this

You would never know we were meant to be forever.

Time may fade the spark in your eyes

The playful breeze may fail to come

Your scented hair may cease to cascade soothingly over my face

The gleaming moon may desert us

No longer to caress us with its golden quill

But I know after these moments pass us,

You will never let my heart be alone

You will never stop listening to the songs

To the voice that holds us in its depths

A voice to strum my heart,

A voice to make me sing forever

Photo/Custom Message

Long before ever I had known you,
There was a time in my life
When the meadows and valleys,
And all in-between listened to my music
 Within all they were they believed in me
They saw the magic of the music
     Wake the birds
     Rise up the Sun
     Stir the breeze
     Unlock the buds
     Move the flowers to dance
They were Amazed when the music brought
Rain clouds from far way.

Meadows and valleys and all in-between were jubilant
Bees and beetles hummed along with the songs
Grasshoppers danced on the leaves, played on grass blades
Dragonflies and butterflies forgot their foes

Long before ever I had known you,
Trees fed me
Clouds sheltered me
Mountain streams stayed still for me to swim
Sparrows and lovebirds watched over me

But, *as always*

Time is impulsive

No one could have seen the dreary wind that was to blow

Over the meadows and valleys and all in-between bringing clouds of grief.

Even the cheer of flowers couldn't stop the tears to come

Sweet honey droplets spilling

Couldn't remove the bitterness, the pain looming below.

Long before ever I had known you,

The long winter brought a late Spring

The late spring brought flowers flourishing to magic music

Never thinking of wilting they danced and laughed as if no end

Swiftly, rolling hills meadows, valleys

And all in between covered in flowers

Fragrance filled everywhere

Winds from distant lands swirling to carry it home

 And yet, no green was to be seen anywhere

The grass and leaves were gone

Beetles, grasshoppers and all bugs struggled to breathe

Beetles, grasshoppers and all bugs prayed

They all prayed for my reed to end its music

At my feet they prayed for my music to die

Heartbroken

Miserable for failing to find a way to console them

I answered their prayers

I did not do as they prayed

> *"If there is no music*
>
> *Meadows, valleys, and everything in between will turn barren*
>
> *The rhythm, the beat of music vibrates within us all*
>
> *Without it the living will cease to exist*
>
> *Like your breath, music makes me live"*

I played and played the reed

My reed played and played the songs that no one ever heard

The screech of the bugs filled the air
Beetles and grasshoppers shrieked to life
Their tears filled the empty rain clouds hovering above.
Unable to hold the pain any longer
Rain began to drop
It rained even through my eyes
I couldn't stop, but I kept playing the reed.
Salty raindrops began to fall into the holes of the reed
Gradually filling the reed
With all my strength I played the reed filled with tears
Churning out silent songs
The agony of a dried up tear duct
Like a quivering womb holding onto a stillborn

Tears of Beetles, grasshoppers and the bugs silenced the reed.
Music stopped
Its silence swallowed vibrations from every life
Orphaned silenced spirits wandered alone
Stifled reed fell
Like the spell of death
It felt as if life was leaving me forever
I dropped exhausted over the flowers

How long I slept? I will never know
But I know I had been in a dream
When I awakened to the touch of the girl from my dream
She was lovelier than any flower ever blossomed
In the breeze her silky long scented hair kept kissing me
Her voice was sweeter than one could ever imagine
Like a flower she danced
Every breath of her
Captured in the air was a flawless fragrance

When I opened my eyes
There was not a single flower to be seen
Meadows, valleys, and everything over it
Carpeted with green grass
Its blades twirled to hug the beetles
And the hoping grass hoppers
Reed was lying near me

No more, it looked heavier
Stains from tears had gone
I took a deep breath and blew into it
But no music was left in it
I looked around for her, but she was not to be seen
I pressed my ear on the ground listening for her footsteps
Heard nothing but the cheers from the life below
She was there for real
The scent I breathed in my dream lingered around me

With untiring eyes searching

Angst-filled heart drifting to merge

I followed the trail of fragrance she left behind

Crossing hills and rivers

Passing through unknown lands

With my mind riding the dawn of hope,

Beating the heat of despair

What I saw next is what made me believe

I was still in a dream.

No mind can reckon

No words can express

No artist's brush strokes can capture that beauty.

My heart skipped its beats

My eyes forgot to blink

Like a stone I froze to the earth.

A tiny village in the midst of mountains

Transcending deep blue lake in the center

Every inch covered in mesmerizing flowers

Every home, its walls and roofs wrapped in flowers

Arching flowers shaded streets and walkways

The air sweetened by honey

Ecstatic bees chanting eternal hymns of love

Baby faced butterflies flew from flower to flower like fairies

With bright petals of clouds around

The Sun looked like a giant sunflower

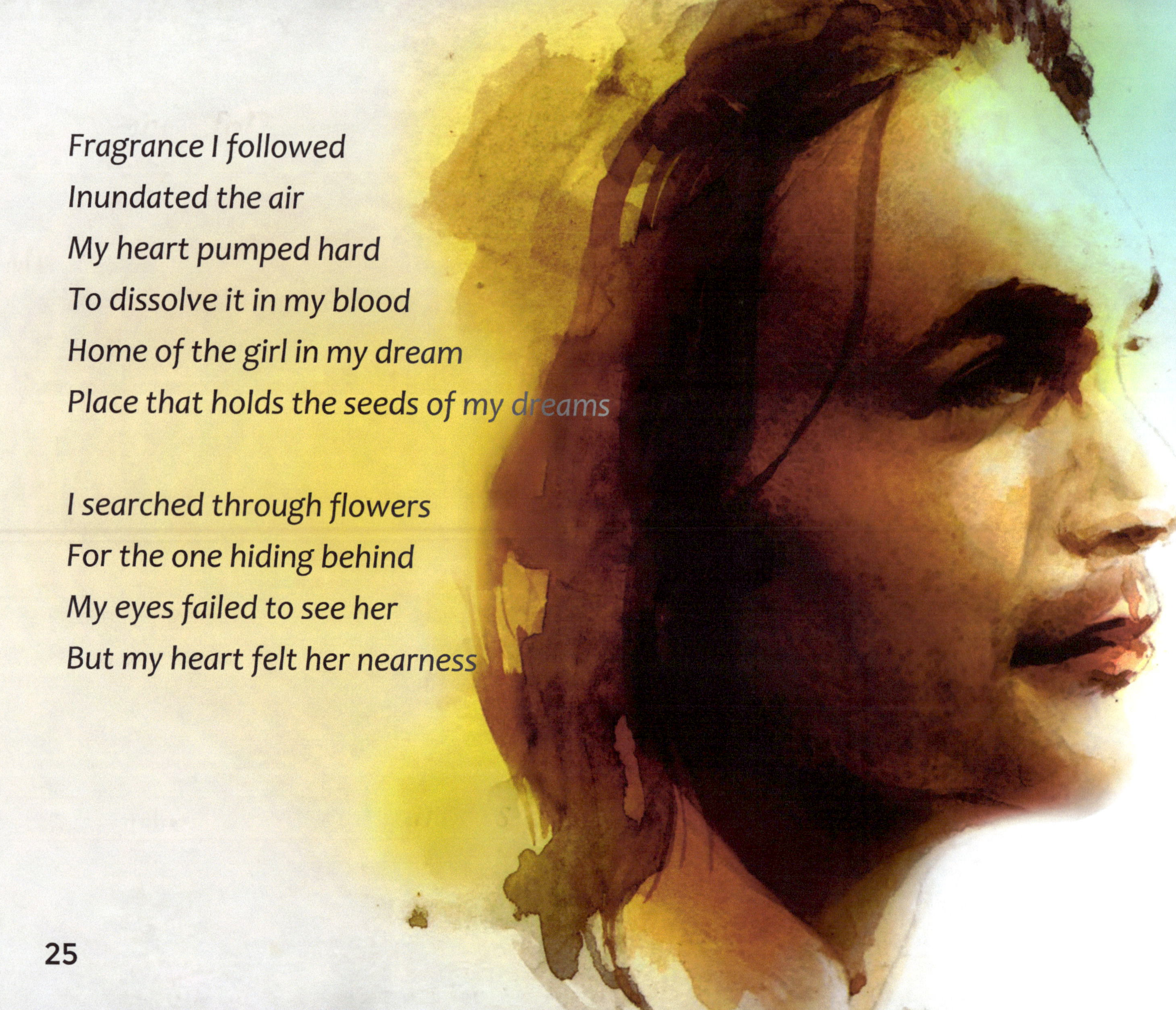

Fragrance I followed
Inundated the air
My heart pumped hard
To dissolve it in my blood
Home of the girl in my dream
Place that holds the seeds of my dreams

I searched through flowers
For the one hiding behind
My eyes failed to see her
But my heart felt her nearness

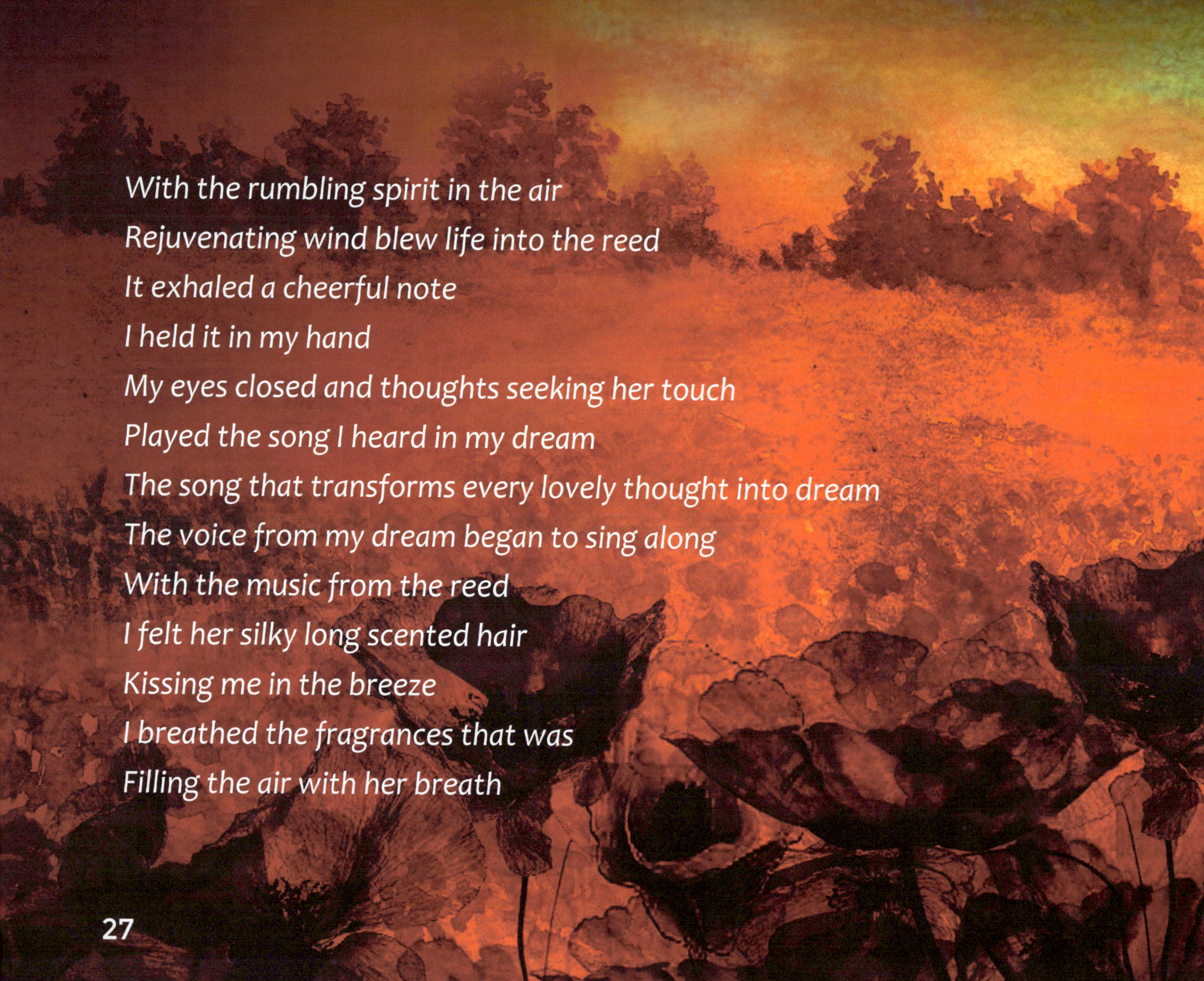

With the rumbling spirit in the air
Rejuvenating wind blew life into the reed
It exhaled a cheerful note
I held it in my hand
My eyes closed and thoughts seeking her touch
Played the song I heard in my dream
The song that transforms every lovely thought into dream
The voice from my dream began to sing along
With the music from the reed
I felt her silky long scented hair
Kissing me in the breeze
I breathed the fragrances that was
Filling the air with her breath

When the music was over

In the stillness of the silence

I opened my eyes

"My love, I saw you standing before me

I touched your silky long scented hair that was kissing me in the breeze

I stood breathing the fragrances of your breath"

The End

Photo/Custom Message
30

ISBN: 978-1-950399-09-3
LCCN: 2021937462